READER-
J

MAYER

Mayer, Mercer

We love you, Lit-
tle Critter!

DUE DATE

A NOTE TO PARENTS

Congratulations on choosing the best in educational materials for your child. By selecting our top-quality products, you can be assured that the concepts used in our books will reinforce and enhance the skills that are being taught in classrooms nationwide.

And what better way to get young readers excited than with Mercer Mayer's Little Critter, a character loved by children everywhere? Our First Readers offer simple and engaging stories about Little Critter that children can read on their own. Each level incorporates reading skills, colorful illustrations, and challenging activities.

Level 1 – The stories are simple and use repetitive language. Illustrations are highly supportive.
Level 2 - The stories begin to grow in complexity. Language is still repetitive, but it is mixed with more challenging vocabulary.
Level 3 - The stories are more complex. Sentences are longer and more varied.

To help your child make the most of this book, look at the first few pictures in the story and discuss what is happening. Ask your child to predict where the story is going. Then, once your child has read the story, have him or her review the word list and do the activities. This will reinforce vocabulary words from the story and build reading comprehension.

You are your child's first and most influential teacher. No one knows your child the way you do. Tailor your time together to reinforce a newly acquired skill or to overcome a temporary stumbling block. Praise your child's progress and ideas, take delight in his or her imagination, and most of all, enjoy your time together!

School Specialty
Children's Publishing

Text Copyright © 2004 School Specialty Children's Publishing. Published by Gingham Dog Press, an imprint of School Specialty Children's Publishing, a member of the School Specialty Family.
Art Copyright © 2004 Mercer Mayer.

Send all inquiries to:
School Specialty Children's Publishing
8720 Orion Place
Columbus, OH 43240-2111

Printed in the United States of America.
1-57768-587-3

 A Big Tuna Trading Company, LLC/J. R. Sansevere Book

3 4 5 6 7 8 9 10 PHXBK 09 08 07 06 05 04

FIRST READERS

Level **1**   Grades **PreK–K**

WE LOVE YOU, LITTLE CRITTER!

TO:
MY BIG BROTHER
FROM:
LITTLE
SISTER

by Mercer Mayer

GINGHAM DOG
P R E S S

Columbus, Ohio

I love my dad.
I help him fix things.

4

5

I love my mom.
I paint pictures for her.

7

I love my little sister.
We play.

I love my grandma.
I sing songs to her.

I love my grandpa.
We go fishing together.

I love my dog.
I take care of him.

15

I love my whole family.
And they love me, too!

17

Word List

Read each word in the lists below. Then, find it in the story. Now, make up a new sentence using the word. Say your sentence out loud.

Words I Know	Challenge Words
dad	family
dog	grandma
help	grandpa
mom	paint
my	pictures
sister	together

Beginning Sound of L

Point to each picture that has the same beginning sound as the word love.

Capitalization: Beginning of a Sentence

The first letter of a sentence always begins with a capital letter.

Example: We love the zoo.

Look at each sentence below. Point to the letter that should be capitalized.

i love my dog.

pink is my mom's favorite color.

my dad is nice.

today, Grandpa went fishing.

The Critter Family

Read the names of Little Critter's family below. Point to the picture of each family member as you read the name.

Mom	Little Sister	Grandma
Dad	Little Critter	Grandpa
	Blue	

Action Match

Action words tell us what is happening.

Example: Little Critter runs.

Read each action word in the left column. Then, point to its matching picture in the right column.

sing

play

fix

paint

Words and Letters

Read the story again. Touch each word with your finger as you read. Then, come back to this page. Use a separate sheet of paper to answer the questions below.

How many words are on page 9?

Which words on page 6 have 3 letters?

Which word on page 11 has 7 letters?

What is the second word on page 14?

Challenge: How many words are in the whole story?

Answer Key

page 19
Beginning Sound of L

lamp

ladder

leaf

lion

lock

log

page 20
Capitalization: Beginning of a Sentence

I love my dog.
Pink is my mom's favorite color.
My dad is nice.
Today, Grandpa went fishing

page 21
The Critter Family

Grandpa   Grandma

Mom

Little Critter

Dad

Little Sister

Blue

page 22
Action Match

fix

play

sing

paint

page 23
Words and Letters

How many words are on page 9? 7
Which words on page 6 have 3 letters? mom, for, her
Which word on page 11 has 7 letters? grandma
What is the second word on page 14? love
Challenge: How many words are in the whole story? 61

24